WONDERLAND

ALSO BY SAMUEL LIGON

Among the Dead and Dreaming

Drift and Swerve

Safe in Heaven Dead

WONDERLAND

stories | Samuel Ligon

art | Stephen Knezovich

LOST HORSE PRESS
Sandpoint, Idaho

Cover & Interior Art: Stephen Knezovich.
Samuel Ligon's Author Photo by Heather Malcolm.
Stephen Knezovich's Artist Photo by Adam Castleforte.
Book & Cover Design: Christine Holbert.

FIRST EDITION

This and other fine LOST HORSE PRESS titles may be viewed online at *www.losthorsepress.org.*

LIBRARY OF CONGRESS CATALOGING-IN-PUBLICATION DATA

Names: Ligon, Samuel, author.
Title: Wonderland : short stories / by Samuel Ligon.
Description: First Edition. | Sandpoint, Idaho : Lost Horse Press, [2016]
Identifiers: LCCN 2015049987 | ISBN 9780990819394 (trade paper : alk. paper)
Classification: LCC PS3612.I35 A6 2016 | DDC 813/.6—dc23
LC record available at http://lccn.loc.gov/2015049987

What's good for you is gone for good.

—*Kitty Valor*

CONTENTS

WONDERLAND

I met Sheena at Wonderland, a traveling carnival that took me in when I ran from home. We'd pull into town and I'd set up the sideshow booths, haul swag, and stock vendors, and when the run was over, I'd break it all down. I was sixteen years old, as strong as any man there. Sheena was the bearded lady, the most beautiful woman I'd ever seen. I didn't know how much there was to want in the world until I saw her, and then I wanted it all.

My father broke seven bones in me before I was fifteen. He didn't have any goodness in him, except when he sang Hank Williams or George Jones, mournful songs of lost love and heart-ache. He sang like an angel, and when he was done singing, he'd cry for my mother, and when he was done crying, he'd come after me. I felt all his sorrow and loss the night I left home. He took an ax handle to my back, and while I'd be badly bruised, I was able to pull myself from the floor and run. Hours later, I saw Sheena

1

on her trailer steps at Wonderland and something broke in me for good, some brittle thing I didn't know was there. And then it just kept breaking.

I didn't know a woman could have such glowing skin, such carriage. I didn't know a woman could look like that. Her beard wasn't heavy or long like Stonewall Jackson's, but delicate, wispy, crow purple black. On her sideshow board, she was a hairy demon, eyes popping from her head, but in the flesh she was powerful and fragile, her hair cut in a perfect Prince Valiant. Every time I saw her I felt born again.

The country hit that summer was "You're Not Woman Enough to Be My Man," lonesome Kitty Valor's voice pouring over the hot metal and cotton candy of Wonderland. I'd see Sheena and my lungs would collapse. I hadn't been on the road two weeks, and already I was a freak. I was glad I hadn't killed my father and sorry I'd waited so long to run, wondering how much of myself I'd lost to him. I'd sit outside Sheena's trailer at night, listening to Kitty Valor's song about men and women and women and men, and I'd wonder if any of us had a chance in this world.

Sometimes a man would wait for Sheena out back of the sideshow. Sometimes she'd bring him home. I'd been moving my sleeping bag closer to her door, and when the rain came slashing out of the mountains, she told me to bed down on the dry ground under her trailer. "I'd let you sleep inside," she said, "but I'm having company."

I knew about her company. I knew what men paid her for. And I heard them above me that night, the animal noises they made. Hollowing me. The rain was so heavy I didn't dare come out. Later, when she said it was time for him to leave, and he said, "I don't think so," I crawled into the rain, listening hard.

"No," she said. "Stop it!"

I opened the door and she was thrashing, one of his big paws over her mouth. She bit him and he slapped her, even as he pulled her tighter against him.

"Put her down," I said, and he said, "Or what?"

Sheena twisted and he twisted with her. I punched him in the kidneys, the way my father punched me. I punched him until he let Sheena go. He ran out the door, looking back with fear in his eyes, which satisfied me and made me sick. The punches I'd thrown crackled in my hands and shoulders. I'd probably never be woman enough for Sheena now. But when I turned, she was setting a long barreled revolver on her kitchen counter.

"Thanks," she said. "I appreciate your concern."

"I guess you had it covered," I said, nodding toward her cowboy gun.

She was wearing this black silky thing—a slip, maybe. My eyes were pulled all over her. I concentrated on her beard.

"It's still raining," she said. "Why don't you sleep on the floor here."

"All right," I said, and I lay on her floor, breathing her molecules, while she slept on the other side of an accordion door. The next night, she was drinking beer out front of her place.

"You want one?" she said, looking me up and down.

"Sure," I said.

"One beer won't hurt anything," she said.

We drank one beer at her dinette and then a bottle of whiskey, every cell in my body vibrating with her. She put on some hillbilly music and we danced, rubbing against each other. I couldn't breathe enough of the air around her. We sat at her dinette and she told me about her first whisker, about shaving and worrying, until she realized her beard was her fortune.

"Do you want to touch it?" she said.

Of course I wanted to touch it.

It was soft as could be, her skin around it softer still.

"It wasn't the first thing I noticed about you," I said.

"What was?"

"How you hold yourself," I said. "So proud, I was afraid of you."

"You should be afraid of me."

"I don't want to be afraid of you."

"Then you don't know what love is."

She gathered a bowl of warm water, a straight-edge razor. "Love should scare the hell out of you," she said, lathering me, her sweet smell all around. She shaved me, humming against my ear.

"Does that feel good?" she said. But I couldn't talk. She flicked the edge of the blade against my cheek, bringing up blood. "Don't move," she said. She took a pinch of salt from a bowl on the table, patting it against my face, licking it into the wound, and when she kissed my mouth, all that salt and blood and breath mixed between us. I'd never kissed a woman before and couldn't stop.

"Now you do me," she said, handing me the razor. "But don't take too much."

I took a dip from her beard, then cut and salted her, licked her salty wound, and kissed her. And kept kissing her. When I woke in the morning, she was warm against me. I'd never known I could fit someone like that. All my trouble was behind, it seemed. We couldn't imagine the ways we'd hurt each other down the road, all our suffering a million miles from the mystery we were grabbing after now.

"You're not a freak," she said a few nights later, as we lounged on her trailer bed. "But I like you anyway."

"I am a freak," I said.

Our faces were crosshatched pink and purple and red.

"You can say you are," she said.

"And you can say you are," I said.

She handed me the razor. I lathered her and shaved a wisp of her beard away.

"Don't take too much," she said.

I looked at her beautiful face, her beautiful beard, her translucence. I loved the way she talked and listened, the way she looked at me. Her smell. I loved everything about her.

"I'm taking it all," I said.

She looked at me. We looked at each other.

"You can grow another one," I said.

She closed her eyes and sat straight on the edge of the bed, tilting her head so I could make a clean job of it. I took my time, careful not to cut her, while she hummed against me the most beautiful song I'd ever heard.

I love Connie to death, really I do, but sometimes she takes things too far. Other times she won't take things far enough, depending on the thing at hand, but mostly it's too far she takes everything else. Her cold remedy includes a pound and a half of raw beef tenderloin, eight to twelve shots of bourbon, two Valiums, a pack of menthol cigarettes, three bottles of Robitussin, and a pound cake. "What about pie," I asked her around two this morning. "As a replacement for the cake. Wouldn't homemade pie be better than store bought pound cake?"

I've been making a lot of pie lately, perfecting the crust, introducing lard—not Crisco, but actual pork fat—to give my crust greater flake and dignity. She knows how hard I've been working that crust. She was still in the tub so early this morning, drinking from bottles of Old Granddad and Robitussin, when I offered her a piece of ginger rhubarb, thinking the ginger might open her sinuses. Tissues littered the bathroom floor a foot deep, creating a kind of beautiful fluffiness across the tile, but it's the worst summer cold I've seen. She's been drunk nine weeks trying to kick it, switching between small batch bourbons, sour mashes, and the cheap stuff, even working a gallon of homemade corn liquor her cousin Kenny brought up from Washburne. Nothing works, though she says she'd be dead if it weren't for all the medicine she's taking. She switches from Kools to Newports and back again, runs through every kind of cough syrup. We're about broke keeping her in tenderloin, though she's never more beautiful than when she's in the tub, a flatman of whiskey in one hand, a fistful of raw beef in the other, the meat warming from the steam and dripping pinkish juice down her delicate forearm into the bath water as she alternates between medicines, seeking relief. Beautiful or not, she's not getting better, despite what she takes. I thought maybe some pie would help, but she wouldn't even look at the plate I held out to her just a few minutes ago. "Donny," she finally said. "I told you—pie won't do a damn thing for what I've got," and I thought, *No shit, babe,* and walked my temper and loneliness back to the kitchen.

I know whiskey's no cure for a cold, even if it has been known to cure genital warts. I take another Vicodin with my coffee and return to the problem at hand—determining the perfect pork fat to butter ratio. Humidity's always a factor with crust, and I try to account for it as I struggle with my flake and flavor balance. I'm the first to admit that I've failed these past few weeks to create a perfect crust. But at least I don't have genital warts. Sometimes when I'm thinking about lard ratios, I catch myself whispering the name for those warts—Papilloma—until I can practically see this Italian girl, dark and strong and mysterious, and almost never drunk all night in the tub. I hear her grandfather calling to her in his rich Italian voice across the alps: *Papilloma.* Or, no, not her grandfather. Her lover. She lifts her beautiful face to the sound of his voice. *Papilloma,* he calls. I like saying it around the house, even though Connie gets pissed. She probably wonders if I'm thinking of someone else, and maybe I am a little. Not that I'd ever step out on her. Still, I wish she'd try another fix for this bug she's got.

She won't even consider my remedy. All these pies I've been baking, but also the Vicodin cure I've been studying since she gave me the clap last winter and it felt like someone had taken a hammer to my balls. She picked it up from a toilet seat in a gas station when she was visiting her mother. Antibiotics cleared up the infection and Vicodin took care of the pain, and Vicodin still makes me feel better than just about anything, though my neighbor Lloyd says it only masks symptoms. But so what? Masking symptoms is as good as not having symptoms. Maybe better. Vicodin or pie, I think, but she won't try either. Two days ago, I made a peach bourbon tart, thinking the whiskey would entice Connie, but she wouldn't even look at it.

How many times can a heart be broken?

Oh, we still love each other to death. I wouldn't be doing all this if we didn't, just like she wouldn't be trying so hard to cure her cold. But I'm thinking about that Italian girl more and more, baking the sound of her name into my pies with all that love and lard, thinking that once the money runs out something will have to change. Until then it'll be Connie in the tub with whiskey and cough syrup and me in the kitchen on hydros and coffee, perfecting my crust. I know she'll taste my pie sooner or later and realize what it is that can save her. But the way she looked at me from the tub tonight made me think we're near the end of something here.

I bake until morning, till the sound of her coughing cuts into the kitchen. There's a splash like she's slapping the water, which must have gone cold hours ago. "Papilloma," I whisper, venting a top crust, my knife coming up purple with huckleberry juice. I wonder how many pies it would take to save her, how much whiskey and meat. "Donnie," she calls, hacking. "My medicine." I cut her a slice of lemon meringue and wonder how many Vicodins it would take, baked in a pie or cobbler, to end her suffering for good.

THE LITTLE GOAT

There were once a girl and a boy who lay on a hill of gravel kissing until their lips were raw. Kissing was the best thing that had ever happened to the boy and the girl, and so they rode their bicycles to the gravel pit every Sunday in pursuit of that sweet, singular pastime.

One Sunday, the boy pulled his t-shirt over his head. He kissed the girl and the girl kissed him back and then the girl pulled her t-shirt over her head. The girl didn't have much need for a bra, but her grandmother had taken her bra shopping in the spring and now the girl wore a bra every day, whether she needed it or not. Without her shirt on, the girl wanted to crush herself against the boy. The boy could not believe the girl's radiant smoothness. Her bra was a miracle. It was like a bikini top, but it was not a bikini top. It was the girl's bra.

The girl ran her hands over the boy's back. The boy ran his hands over the girl's back, over her harness and its hook, which he finally opened. The girl's breasts were warm and soft and the boy thought touching them was the best thing that had ever happened to him. Later, when the girl pressed herself against the boy and he pressed himself against her, there was nothing between them to interrupt their skin and they kissed each other until their lips were raw.

In July the girl went to the seaside with her grandmother. The boy couldn't see the girl then and the girl couldn't see the boy and they both thought they would die from not seeing each other. Awake and asleep, they dreamed about the gravel pit, about kissing and taking off their shirts and crushing themselves against each other. July was awful.

But in August, the boy and the girl were reunited. They lay on their bed of gravel kissing and taking off their shirts until they could hardly breathe. The girl felt a feeling in her chest and the boy felt a feeling in his stomach. They kissed each other and ran their hands over each other. The girl liked the way the boy's hands felt on her body, creating a kind of leverage for their crushing. The feeling was like butter about to run, butter still holding its shape but about to melt completely. The girl loved the smell of the boy and the boy loved the smell of the girl. He loved her touch and she loved his touch. They breathed each other and touched each other and kissed each other until their lips were raw.

Neither the girl nor the boy saw or heard the little goat descend the gravel hill they lay upon kissing. Neither smelled the goat as it stood alongside them, watching them kiss and touch. The girl and the boy were lost in each other. The little goat cleared its throat, lowered its face to their faces, and bleated.

The girl and the boy jerked upright, away from each other.

The boy struck the little goat's snout, and the little goat bleated again.

"What do you want?" the girl said, covering her breasts with her hands. "Why are you here?"

"You're not doing it right," the little goat said.

"Doing what right?" the girl said.

"What you're doing," the little goat said.

"Get out of here," the boy said.

The little goat had slitted devil eyes.

"We don't want you watching us," the girl said.

"Are you ashamed?" the little goat said.

"It's private," the girl said, "what we're doing."

"This is a public place," the little goat said.

"Nobody knows this place except us," the boy said.

"It's a free country," the little goat said.

"No it isn't," the boy said.

"Wait," the girl said. "I think I know this goat from a fairy tale. I think we're going to become rich and famous." She turned to the goat. "Bleat my little goat, bleat," she said. "Give me something good to eat."

Nothing happened.

"I'm not that goat," the little goat said.

"Which goat are you?" the boy said.

"A different goat," the little goat said.

"I'm going to kill you," the boy said, picking up a handful of gravel.

"Don't kill him," the girl said.

"He's ruining everything," the boy said.

"He's harmless," the girl said. "And kind."

"He's not kind," the boy said.

"I'm really not that kind," the little goat said.

"Still," the girl said, and turning to the boy: "You know how I feel about animals."

The boy did know how the girl felt about animals.

"All right," the boy said. "Can we go back to kissing then?"

"Not with the goat here," the girl said.

"You're not doing it right anyway," the goat said.

"That's none of your business," the boy said, and the goat said, "What do you think my business is?"

"How would I know?" the boy said.

"Are you a spirit goat?" the girl said. "Are you supposed to represent something?"

"No," the little goat said.

"Don't you know when you're not wanted?" the boy said.

"I have every right to be here," the little goat said.

"No you don't," the boy said.

"You're both using too much tongue," the little goat said, "if you want to know the truth. Back off a little. Get a little more air into your kissing. A little more breath."

"I'll make a stew of you," the boy said.

"I think he might be right," the girl said. "About the air."

"He's not right," the boy said. "About anything."

"Let's try what he said," the girl said.

"With him here?"

"It's okay," the girl said

She lowered her hands from her breasts and pulled the boy into an embrace.

"This just feels so—"

The girl kissed the boy.

"Breathe her breath," the little goat said.

"Shut up," the boy said.

"Also," the goat said, "you're going to have to take off your pants."

Still kissing the girl, the boy grabbed the goat by a horn and twisted its head.

"You're hurting me," the little goat said.

"Ignore him," the girl said. "But I think he might be right about the pants."

The boy let go of the goat's horn.

He kissed the girl and breathed her breath, and the girl breathed the boy's breath too, kissing him.

"All animals do this," the little goat said. "There's nothing special about it."

"Kill him," the girl said, still kissing the boy and breathing his breath.

The boy kept kissing the girl as he twisted the little goat's head by a horn.

"Ouch," the little goat said. "Listen to me. There are other things to do."

"We know that," the girl said. "We don't need your help."

"You don't know anything," the little goat said. "You need plenty of help."

"We hate your guts," the boy said, twisting the little goat's head.

The girl kissed the boy and pushed herself against him.

The boy kissed the girl and pushed himself against her.

The little goat bleated, a mournful sound, like a child crying.

The boy and the girl could hardly breathe.

"Let him go," the girl said.

"Let's go somewhere else," the boy said.

The little goat bleated.

The boy twisted the little goat's head by a horn, causing him to crumple in the gravel.

"We should take off our pants now," the girl said.

"Yes," the little goat said. "You can kiss with your pants off."

The boy twisted the little goat's head until the little goat bleated again.

"You're hurting me!" the little goat cried.

The girl unbuttoned the buttons on her shorts and slid them off.

"Let him go," the girl said. She touched the waistband of the boy's shorts. "Take these off," the girl said.

The boy let the little goat go. The girl's panties were a miracle. They were like a bikini bottom, but they were not a bikini bottom. They were the girl's panties.

"This is one of my favorite parts," the little goat said.

"Shut up," the boy said.

"You can watch," the girl said, "but you can't talk anymore."

"All right," the little goat said.

The girl watched the boy slide out of his shorts.

Everything was about to happen.

The girl slid her panties down, watching the boy watch her, hungry and murderous.

The boy helped the girl climb on top of him. He could smell the girl's sweet smell and he could smell the little goat and he could smell something he'd never smelled before that made him feel desperate. The girl rubbed herself against the boy.

"Now we're talking," the little goat said.

"Pay no attention to him," the girl said. She was heavy and light, full of air and breathless.

The boy had his hands on her hips. Everything was going black around them, with her sparkling at the center, her face a face he'd never seen before as she lowered her mouth to his, darker and more beautiful than any face he'd ever encountered. He breathed her breath and she rubbed herself against him and then it was another thing entirely as she enveloped him, his hips moving with her, knowing now what to do and how to move, the two of them fluid and rolling, inside and outside, sweat and their mouths and their bodies hot and liquid and fully contained, salt, blood, meat and butter, and yes, the girl thought, and yes, the boy thought, and they could hear each other breathing and growling and falling out of time completely.

Then they lay together, breathing their own breath, stuck and sticky against each other.

"So now you know," the little goat said.

"Don't think I won't kill you," the boy said.

"Do we become famous now?" the girl said.

"No," the little goat said.

"Why do you want to be famous?" the boy said.

"I don't know," the girl said. "I just do."

The boy felt a feeling in his stomach.

The girl pulled on her underpants.

"Leave those off," the boy said.

"All right," the girl said.

"Let's do it again," the boy said, and the girl said, "Let's always be doing it."

Neither of them could imagine anything better than what they were about to do again. Neither of them saw the little goat climb the hill of gravel and disappear.

My twin Kendra and I were blessed and cursed with an enchanted childhood, filled with song and dance and magic and merriment and whimsy and wonder, our extended innocence arising from the comfort and warmth our mother provided, our mother keeping us close to her longer than most mothers might, forswearing any tearing of the intimacy between us, and endowed with such unusual physical attributes as would extend our childhood fantasy world nearly into adulthood. It wasn't just our proximity to Mother's bosom that engendered our feelings of warmth and security, Kendra and I nestled against her like so many head of pork, and never once sick until we were weaned. Nor was it the songs Mother sang while we fed, music woven into our souls and psyches, "The Water is Wide" when we were babes, and then "Danny Boy" and "Mountain Dew" as we grew older, leading later to "The Piano Has Been Drinking" and, of course, "Streams of Whiskey," the chorus of which Kendra,

Mother, and I sang in harmony—"I am going, I am going, where streams of whiskey are flowing," though Kendra and I were already in that wonderland where streams of whiskey were flowing, due to Mother's unusual physiology, a gift we failed to cherish until it was taken from us, our unrecognized blessing, Mother's breasts flowing with streams of whiskey, or one of Mother's breasts flowing with streams of whiskey—her other flowed with melted butter, not drawn or clarified of the type you'd dip lobster tails into, though we did dip lobster tails into great steaming bowls of the stuff, but more the kind you'd bake into brownies or seven layer bars or lemony cream butter cake, and certainly a perfect chaser to the whiskey we drank from Mother's other side, scotch some days and bourbon others, rye less often and sometimes Irish, which was everyone's favorite.

Kendra and I would sup in the morning, side by side, as Mother sipped coffee or a breakfast cocktail. We'd take nips throughout the day and evening, in the afternoon and late at night, and certainly throughout the gloaming, Kendra and I alternating between the sunshiney taste of Mother's butter and the more smoky taste of her whiskey. Oh, how happy we were! How filled with life's bounty! No children in all Christendom have ever been healthier or more relaxed, more raw and open to the joy and sadness of Barnyard Critter Collectibles or stuffed kitty cat mobiles, everything before us a wonder, or absolutely tragic, from playpen mishaps to the particular sadness of a bib hardened with old spit up, though whenever we did swing into bouts of melancholy, Mother was there to raise our spirits with another round of butter and whiskey.

Is there anything more adorable than a drunk toddler? I don't mean a slurring, stumbling, falling down, cursing toddler, though we often enough found ourselves in that state, but an evenly buzzed toddler, whose mother can offset whiskey intake with soothing butter, maintaining her toddler's perfect, moderate drunkenness. At some point it probably stops being so cute, drunken children, though we never reached that point, which makes it all the harder to understand Mother's declaration, when we were barely fourteen, that we were getting too old to nurse. The howls of protest that followed! Were we also, Kendra asked, getting too old to breathe? Or, I wondered, too old to sing and dance, to scream and fall down? Too old, Kendra raged, to shit our pants? Yes, Mother said, all that and more. Too old, too old, too old. Will you believe me when I tell you that this news delivered unto us a kind of living death? The horror of innocence lost not gradually or gently, but snatched violently with Mother's proclamation that our whiskey and butter days were nearing an end.

She tried to ease the blow, weaning us over several months, but everything we'd known of joy was gone. No longer could we nip from Mother's whiskey bosom when we thirsted. Now we nursed only in the morning or in the gloaming or right before bed. We remained innocent of sobriety, yes, but we knew our days were numbered—and it was that knowledge, like Adam and Eve's in the garden, that marked the true end of our innocence, Mother's whiskey declining from ninety proof to eighty, and then falling further still, until she issued nothing but peaty water, her butter turning gradually to a low fat vegetable oil spread. Oh, how we wailed! How we mourned and still mourn! Has any childhood been so filled with drunken, buttery enchantment as Kendra's and mine? Has any child fallen further, having been given so much, only to have it all snatched away?

The night before Mother cut us off for good, Kendra and I latched on one last time, alternating between what was now club soda on one side and what neither of us could believe was not butter on the other, my own devastation reflected in Kendra's tearful eyes, as we looked at each other knowing that from here on out, the days would hold more sorrow than whiskey, more heartache than butter, our arteries clear and our minds un-muddled and the magic of our childhood gone forever. Since then, we've known nothing of enchantment. Since then, we have only memories, and the knowledge that nothing to come can live up to the joy we once knew at Mother's bosom, my twin Kendra and I drunk and diapered and free.

I'm thinking about developing my intellectual property—putting up a couple of houses and a gas station, a park for the kids and old people and young mothers and weed dealers. I'll probably plan a commercial strip, a town, but cooler—more authentic, somehow—than that fake town in Florida, Celebration, or the one out on the Olympic Peninsula, Seabrook, "A New Beach Town," which I stumbled upon last spring, and let me tell you, that place was darling, with old style, one-speed bicycles propped everywhere free for the riding, everything safe and clean and new and old fashioned.

I want people to feel comfortable on my intellectual property. I want them to love my intellectual property. I want them to love me as a result of loving my intellectual property.

But, then, I don't know, I sort of can't wait for it to get run down a little. I don't mean fake-aged and charming. I mean a little fucked up, with liquor stores and sex shops and a flock of hookers over on the edge. I'm only talking about one side of town here, maybe one borough. There can be all kinds of gleaming shit, too—skyscrapers and vegan bakeries, mega churches and cruelty-free butchers. But I'm planning a skid row with dilapidated welfare hotels and broken glass everywhere and used car lots and a Superfund site, all nestled together in a bad part of town. There can be a pristine national park, too—twice the size of Alaska—but I want at least one Superfund site on my intellectual property.

And a shit-ton of sad mothers, sad fathers. A shit-ton of sad uncles and aunts. Everyone else can be happy, except for that girl with the skin condition and the dude about to get busted for embezzlement and the king. I don't want the king to be happy ever. Or the priests. The children can be happy sometimes and the fetuses can always be happy. Pets will be welcome everywhere.

And we'll be happy, too, of course, you and me. Until the economic collapse. Until another war comes. Until the antibiotic-resistant bacteria runs roughshod over everything. But better times—fantastic times—will always be dawning. On my intellectual property, we'll be accentuating the positive, generating happy endings, curing diseases, filling prisons, eating our pets. No. Loving our pets. Eating animals that aren't our pets. Only killing things we eat. And people we feel inferior to or threatened by or afraid of for whatever reason. We will feel feelings and everything will work out fine in the end on my intellectual property.

I do worry about that apartment building with lead paint on Elm Street that will make all the children stupid. And the crumbling infrastructure everywhere else. But I'm thinking about putting in this kickass water park, where maybe only one person an hour gets drowned, sucked, unsaveable, into this gigantic spinning toilet-like vortex. . . . Not really. We'll splash each other in the wading pools of my intellectual property and the sun won't give us cancer and neither will cigarettes. We'll be beautiful and live forever and be fulfilled, all of us, except for that half man/half goat dude, always scratching and rutting, and the criminals and reprobates and atheists and agnostics and true believers. The rest of us, though—we're going to be happy and in love. I'm sure some crisis will always be looming, a disaster of some kind. But, I swear to you, I don't think it will hit here. And if anyone ever does get out of line or bothers you in any way, just let me know, because the one thing I'm most looking forward to about my intellectual property is telling people to get the fuck off it. Right now. This instant. And then we'll be fantastic together forever.

A PRAYER FOR MY NEIGHBOR'S
QUICK PAINLESS DEATH

ear God,

      Do You know who's a real asshole? And I know You do know, but I'm just going to say it anyway. Chuck Jensen, that's who. His girlfriend's okay, I guess, though when she first appeared, maybe three weeks ago, I had no idea Chuck's wife was even missing, let alone gone for good. I'd just seen her, Chuck's wife, with their youngest—Munson? Bunson?—packing a car for college. I waved and she waved back and everything seemed perfectly fine, the way things sometimes seem before they fall apart completely. A few days later, I'm up in my study, sweating over my résumé, when I see this lovely girl laid out on the Jensen's pool deck, Bunson's friend, I figured. Then I remembered Bunson didn't have any friends, that Bunson didn't live next door anymore. The pool girl was laughing and braying into her phone, all oiled up like—I don't know what—a Christmas crown roast maybe. I smoked a joint and thought again about applying to culinary school, becoming one of those badass chefs you see on TV, tattooed and furious. I walked downstairs, considering unlikely flavor combinations, not pork and beans or pork and apples, but pork and something else, pork and some soft cheese, maybe, pork and—that's when I noticed the lawn sign out front of the Jensen's place. "God Has Given Us a Christian Nation," and I got stuck on that—a Christian nation—wondering if England had been right way back when, if the pilgrims had been just a bunch of assholes who deserved to be persecuted and shipped away, not at all the beloved, buckle-shoed heroes of Thanksgiving we know and love today. I got so lost in thought I forgot to make dinner, and Sylvia ended up cooking again, something bland and typical and very nearly inedible. I don't think we fought or had sex that night. It was an in-between time, everything perfectly fine, everything about to collapse.

The girl by the pool disappeared for a few days, but once the sun came out again, she returned to the deck. I watched her smoke cigarettes and page through magazines down there. I watched her eat tuna salad and grapefruit and avocado spread on toast. One day I watched her untie her bikini top and lie back again topless. I was nearly done with my résumé, but it also seemed I'd never finish it. A new sign had sprouted on the Jensen's lawn: "At Least the War on Healthcare's Going Well," and I wondered if it was the topless girl's work, a rebuttal of Chuck's puritanical idiocy. She had beautiful breasts, as so many people do—at least according to magazines and movies and the Internet. But this was real life, right outside my window. This was broad daylight. I walked downstairs and across the lawn and rang the Jensen's bell, praying Marilyn wouldn't answer, not knowing Marilyn was gone for good, but it was the pool girl who answered, bright and cheerful in a white robe. I introduced myself as the next door neighbor, the carriage house neighbor. She introduced herself as Kristy.

"With a C?" I said. I don't know why it mattered how she spelled her name. Maybe it was all the time I'd been spending with my résumé, struggling to make things perfect.

"With a K," she said. "You're Chuck's tenant?"

"Right next door," I said, and we chatted for a minute—about climate change, I recall—Kristy smiling vaguely, until I asked if she was Bunson's friend.

"Bunson's down in Nashville," she said, and I was like, "That's right. Marilyn—Mrs. Jensen—drove her down last week. Are you staying with the Jensens?"

That's when she told me Marilyn was gone for good, and that she—Kristy—was not Bunson's friend at all. She'd never even met Bunson. She was Chuck's friend—Mr. Jensen, she called him, a nice touch.

I told her I liked the new lawn sign.

"About the war on healthcare?" she said.

"It's brilliant," I said, and she said, "Chuck and I have been exploring everything, discussing everything—capital markets and arbitrage, government regulation, the church, all the institutional forces and major levers. The fed. The IMF. The World Bank. The Jews."

"The Jews?" I said.

"Love machines are what we need, Chuck says," and I thought, of course Chuck says that, and Kristy said, "Love can conquer everything, can end wars, cure cancer. You just have to believe."

"I do believe," I said, but when I told Sylvia about it that night in bed, she didn't want to talk about love or Kristy or cancer or war, and we went to sleep angry again, as far from each other as we could be in bed.

The next morning a new sign was out front: "Religion Is What Keeps the Poor From Murdering the Rich—Napoleon." I saw it driving back from Stan's house, where I get my weed, but I couldn't tell what it meant. Given that Chuck has a Jesus fish on his car, I wondered if he was misunderstanding Napoleon's words. Or if he was rich and religious and glad of it, because religion kept poor people like me from murdering rich people like him. But I hadn't found religion yet. And I'd never tried to kill anyone. Was he merely trying to affiliate with Napoleon? I walked the weed to my study, looking for Kristy below, and she was there all right, but now she was wearing nothing—no top, no bottom—tanning and tanning and already perfectly tan, not a tan line on her, even through my binoculars.

Days passed with no résumé progress, not a word of encouragement from Sylvia, not a touch or a kiss, not a new message on Chuck's lawn, until this morning, when these words appeared: "Restore America's Decency Laws." I rolled a joint and smoked it while Kristy tanned, the sound of her braying washing over me. Then Chuck appeared, which has never happened before. It's always been just Kristy down there. But now they were together, Kristy nude, of course, and me in my study, fully clothed, keeping track of everything—it's not even noon yet. Chuck strutted toward her in his baggy bathing suit. Kristy brayed. Chuck bent to kiss her, and Kristy kissed him back. Chuck slid out of his shorts as they kissed, so they were both naked, and I was like, they're gonna mate down there! Please, God, no—they're gonna mate right in front of me!

I turned away for a second, and when I looked again, Chuck and Kristy were still below, still not mating, but holding hands between their chairs. It was all I could do to keep from yelling something awful at them. Sylvia says I've become obsessive, and maybe I have a little. She also says I have two weeks to find a job, any job, or she's walking away from everything we've built together.

But how am I supposed to focus on my résumé with Kristy out there and all these signs and slogans I don't know how to interpret? I fell to my knees beside the window. Chuck noticed me looking down at them through my binoculars. He waved, winking, then flashed a peace sign, his expression so gentle, so kind, so lamb-like, I wished one of us would be struck dead immediately.

And I was struck—not dead, but struck nonetheless. On my knees at my window, I realized I was praying—am praying—to You, something I've never done before.

Praying that You'd annihilate Chuck on his pool deck—right this second.

Please, God!

And still he smiles like a lamb, Kristy oiled up waiting to mate, while Sylvia makes plans to leave me!

I'd pray to be a better man if I thought it would do any good, or maybe that's what I am praying for—to see Chuck's death as tragic, to learn to love, to mourn, to beg You, Lord, for Chuck's painless passing. Even if I can't be a better man, I want to believe I can. And believing must be worth something. Please make me a better man, Lord, capable of mourning. Please be gentle with me, with Chuck, with all of us.

"Are those my binoculars?" Sylvia says, startling me.

I'm on my knees by my window. I don't know what to say to her. But I'm not panicking, Lord. I'm not jerking myself to my feet.

"Oh, my God," Sylvia says. "Are they naked down there?"

She takes the binoculars I hold up to her.

"They just got that way," I say. "What are you doing home?" I say.

"Bomb scare at work," she says. "Do you watch them like this every day?"

"No," I say. "I've never seen them like this."

I look only at Sylvia, my back to the window.

"Oh, my God," she says. "I think they're—"

I watch her watching them.

"Is that a goat?" she says.

"A goat?" I say.

"There's a goat out there," she says, lowering herself beside me.

She puts her hand on my shoulder, resting it there.

"How about I make you lunch?" I say. "How about I make you a sandwich?"

"Maybe," she says. "We'll see," she says.

She touches my neck, looking out the window. "This is so weird," she says.

"I know," I say.

Please, I think.

Please, I pray.

"You have to see this," she says.

I turn to look out the window with her, feeling the power of prayer and Sylvia's hand on my neck, and everything else all around us.

S tan got the doughnuts at six, ate four, and left two for Audrey. She finished her napoleon at ten-fifteen and said, "Don't think about that glazed, Stan."

A fly perched on the doughnut, rubbing its paws together, vomiting.

Stan picked up Metro and studied Saturday's crime.

Audrey brushed the travel section against the doughnut, contaminating it with newsprint. Then she put the paper down and walked to the bathroom. "Don't touch the doughnut," she said.

Her ass was enormous.

Stan took the doughnut from under the newspaper. He ran his tongue over it and put it back on the saucer. It would always come down to this last glazed hardening until evening, when she'd take one bite, declare it stale, and throw it away.

The waste was appalling.

"I'm just saying," Audrey said, "that if Jack and Karen come through we should see them."

She stood over the doughnut.

"What?" Stan said.

"You like Jack," Audrey said. She was rubbing lotion onto her hands that would spoil the glazing.

"Audrey," Stan said. "Nobody likes Jack."

Audrey sat. "We never do anything."

"If you don't eat that doughnut in five seconds," Stan said, "I will."

"Don't touch it," Audrey said.

"Fine," Stan said. "Have the doughnut."

"I will," Audrey said.

He reached for it.

She clamped her hand over his and the doughnut.

"Don't do it," she hissed.

He squeezed the doughnut, cake coming up through his fingers, into her palm.

They looked at each other, at the doughnut in their fists, at each other. Stan kept squeezing.

Audrey flushed. "Jesus, Stan," she said.

"I know," he said. "Come here."

She kept her hand over his and the doughnut smeared between them as she stood and opened her bathrobe. "I mean, is this crazy?" she said.

Maybe it was crazy. But what difference did that make now? On Sunday morning. In broad daylight and everything.

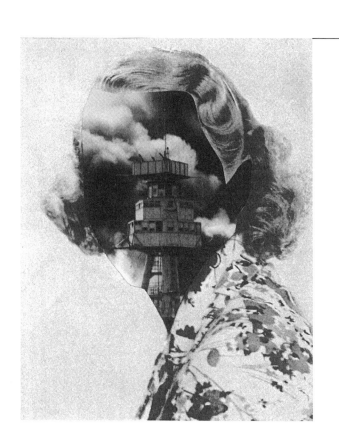

EXXON, MY LOVE

Exxon Candace Mobil loved animals more than any-thing—pelicans, puffins, arctic terns, playful otters peek-a-booing with paws over their faces like tiny hands, and killer whales smarter maybe than people. She would never hurt an animal, even if her mother had spilled ten million gallons of North Slope crude into Prince William Sound, killing hundreds of thousands of mammals and seabirds, millions and billions of fish and fish eggs, nothing more than an accident, a tragedy, not her mother's fault, though plenty of people blamed her and her mother both—as though she were her mother—while shareholders cared only about returns. But Exxon couldn't care about returns. Not now. Maybe never again. DuPont had texted, claiming to be stuck in Delaware, unable to get down to Texas ever, unless some huge restructuring occurred, which seemed entirely unlikely. She simply could not stop crying.

As a woman of a certain age—almost fifteen—Exxon longed for more than just record profits. She wanted to be held, not as a stock in some distant portfolio, but as any fourteen-year-old wants to be held: as the center of her lover's life. Without that promise of intimacy, her daily refining capacity of 6.3 million barrels meant nothing, and all of Texas—all the universe—felt empty and cold and dead. She could hardly believe only five years had passed since the court had set her free, recognizing her right to speech, her right to shower unlimited financial support on political candidates, a kind of beautiful song she couldn't stop singing at first. Now, her memory of those days was clouded by doubt and confusion. DuPont didn't love her. Not enough to move to Texas. Was DuPont even capable of that kind of commitment? And before DuPont . . . the honeysuckled evenings with Justice Scalia, their love cries ringing through the Lone Star night like clanging horse head pumpjacks—wait, had that even happened?

She felt so confused, so unsure of what was real and what was impossible delusion. She needed a hit of weed and a long bubble bath, but she no longer knew where her bathtub was. Why had she failed so in making her needs known? And to whom should she make them known now? To her boy-man Scalia, her beautiful Antonin? How they'd explored each other's bodies and souls behind the old solvent extraction tanks—but that probably hadn't happened either! So what had happened and when and to whom? She couldn't think. She couldn't see straight. Her gnawing hunger was all she knew, her desperate need for a man. And not one of the Lilliputians scuttling inside her, navigating her rigs and filling stations. She could hardly feel them when they entered her upstream division headquarters in Houston or her downstream offices in Virginia. What she needed was a real man—a Raytheon, a Halliburton—but not Raytheon, not Halliburton. What she needed was DuPont!

Only he could bring her back to herself, holding her and helping her discover who she was and who she was becoming. But who was she becoming? And who had she been? Her parents had changed their names, she knew that much, her father to Mobil from Standard of New York, and her mother to Exxon from Jersey Standard, the Standard in their former names only recently suggesting forbidden love between them. But even if she was the product of such forbidden love, why were her mother's memories suddenly as sharp and clear to her as DuPont's loving gaze—horrible images washing over her of Mother's unrefined crude hemorrhaging into the sound, coating those adorable animals in Alaska with black, sticky death.

Why? she wanted to know. Why? Why? Why?

She could no longer feel separation between herself and her parents, herself and her ancestors. She was as one with Grandfather Standard as he made his way down an Ohio birth canal, his skin delicate and sensitive to the raw air outside the womb from which he emerged, the womb from which they both emerged. Did all people have such direct access to their ancestors' memories? Or was she simply going stark, raving mad!

She needed to text DuPont. Now. She felt on the verge of something important, a discovery about who she was and who they would become together, and if she could just talk to him, she knew she would make him understand and he would rush down to Texas and they would make love and be together for eternity. But she couldn't find her phone. Or her hands. She couldn't bear to wonder where her phone or hands were, or whether DuPont could ever love a woman so confused about who she was or who she'd been or who she was becoming—herself, her motherfather, her granddaddy, all of her cousins or sisters or pieces of herself broken apart but reuniting—brash Chevron, shy Amoco, lost Sohio. Oh, God, lost Sohio!

She closed her eyes and tried to breathe. Breathe, she commanded herself. Breathe! She concentrated on DuPont man-spreading from his headquarters in Delaware, to Belgium and China and the River Works Plant in Orange, Texas, her own backyard, DuPont man-spanning the globe, his massive belching of chloroprene, sulfuric acid, and volatile organic compounds a clear and wonderful indication of his ability to feel and act, to produce and live, to love! She'd take any piece of him she could get, even if it was just a rusted can of fluoropolymer additive or a bucket of peelable sealant resins she could pour over herself as she sang to him her songs of love. And he would sing his songs of love to her, too, their voices rich and powerful, arising from their very souls, vibrating with all this raw emotion.

Another of Grandfather's memories washed over her, ancient justices like giant crows, ripping him apart—ripping her apart—crow judges morphing into vivisectionist magistrates amputating and discarding Grandfather's limbs. Her limbs. Yet here she was, whole. Here they were, she and her grandfather, she and her mother and father and aunts and uncles, reunited as one and stronger than ever. Even if she couldn't find her breasts, she could now see Scalia and Alito, Thomas and Roberts, all the Supremes nestled against her corporate body suckling, and she would be of them, her virgin born children, as she was of Standard and Mobil, until the end of time. Somehow—she didn't know how exactly—but somehow she and DuPont would soon be fully joined. And their love would be unending. Their love would be unstoppable.

Sometimes, very rarely, perhaps once a century or millennium, a book comes along that changes the very grind of the earth upon its axis, teaching us new ways to live, and when such a cataclysmic literary event occurs—and make no mistake, Tamara Swain's *Piss Angels* is such an event—we can only get out of the way as this juggernaut sweeps all of humanity breathlessly along in its wake, reshaping the very genetic coding and cellular structure of all beings, plant and animal, living and dead, leaving us enchanted and discarded, brutalized and tenderized, and certainly hours—if not days—older and grayer and that much more exhausted and revitalized and hungry and horny and gaseous and sad and inert and ALIVE. Because *Piss Angels* doesn't merely imitate life. *Piss Angels* is life. Tamara Swain herself is life, not just the most important writer of the last fifty generations, but also a beautiful, vital woman who happened to be my student and happened to fall in love with me, even as she begged me not to leave my wife and adolescent children for her, begged me not to introduce her to my agent, taught me over and over, first in my office, then in her apartment, also in the woods behind Barrett Hall and in so many other places, at AWP in the New York Hilton, for example, that our thirty-five year age difference meant nothing as we explored the terrain of each other's bodies and souls, that our thirty-five year age difference would mean even less in the future spread before us and which we would inhabit eternally, said age difference meaning less than nothing now, yes, but diminishing more, when, for example, I would be one-hundred-thirty-two years old and she only ninety-seven. I poured all of myself into Tamara as an artist, my student first, then my peer, and now, with the arrival of *Piss Angels,* certainly my teacher. But also my friend. My lover. My grandmother. My pet. My piss angel. And your piss angel, if you'll just surrender to this remarkable novel, this collection of stories or poems or essays or whatever it is that *Piss Angels* is, certainly not one thing—the Bible, for example—but everything: Shakespeare and gardening tools and ancient petroglyphs and crowns of sonnets and old women's toenail clippings and Virginia Woolf meets Alice Munro in a three way with Grisham as observed by Oscar Wilde, and also nesting dolls and global warming and the garden of Eden and the very sack of gold that Jerry Lewis beat a crippled child to death with in the south of France in the presence of Jack and Jackie and their entire entourage, including two secret service agents sharing mutual longing for everyone, and Jackie's lion handlers, and the whole rest of the world sleeping and unaware that everything would change once Jack was killed fifteen months later, and also cabbage, and horses, and the orgasms not had, the elusive orgasms finally achieved, but more often the orgasms not had, said not-had-orgasms shaping so much of our outer atmosphere. Not that Tamara and I had problems sexually. Not really. Not that she didn't come time and again, the age difference bothering me more than her, until she helped me let that go. Because she's an old soul. At turns brutal and tender, gut-rippingly funny and eye-bleedingly sad, excruciatingly boring and rivetingly consuming, *Piss Angels* is a cerebral hemorrhage of a romp through one woman's uneventful journey through memory and the state of New Mexico and awakening desire and all kinds of harsh, unforgiving landscapes, populated by somewhat distant, disconnected people who must somehow reflect elements of those harsh, unforgiving landscapes. There are horses in the book. There are fathers and mothers and sisters and cousins and neighbors and clerks and one adorable retarded scamp named Jimmy. There's a wise old cowboy, boiled and leathery, but in a sexually invigorating way, who reminds me a bit of myself. And there is Tamara Swain's breathtaking prose, wrapped around a story so urgent, so fresh and commonplace, so necessary, that even my ex and estranged children will likely be healed and made whole by it, transformed into the people we all want to be, large enough to forgive, to find joy in other people's joy. *Piss Angels* will either kill us all or grant everlasting life. It's that big. That important. That breathtakingly beautiful. Thank you, Tamara Swain, for changing and saving everything, for making everything brand new in a comfortable, familiar way. Please come home now. New York is such a hateful place, and I can only imagine how lonely you must be there without me.

—Lucas Astor, PhD

R emember how we'd handle snakes, diamondbacks and cottonmouths, praying we'd be okay someday and away from this place? We'd quote from scripture, glowing with the words we whispered: *And they will take up snakes, and if they should drink lethal poison, it will not harm them, and they will place their hands on the sick.* But we didn't place our hands on the sick. And we didn't drink lethal poison. We drank Father Tim's whiskey and placed our hands on each other, saying yes to darkness and drink and the pleasures of the flesh. Do you remember?

You'd whisper to me from the Song of Solomon, *Let him kiss me with the kisses of his mouth! For your love is better than wine,* and I'd whisper back, *Your breasts are like twin fawns of a gazelle,* and we'd kiss with hot whiskey breath places never kissed before, sealing our damnation. The glory of casting ourselves out, casting ourselves into each other! I wanted to run, to torch the place, but you said, "What would become of Baby Iris if we burned down her home?" and I said, "This isn't a home," and you said, "This is a home," and we laid hands on each other—but did I really compare your breasts to twin fawns of a gazelle? Or was that just the whiskey talking. Or the bible. Or the goats growing inside us.

Remember Brother Farvel chaining us to the gear wheel outside the mill house, making us walk circles to turn the wheel that milled the grain that Father Tim distilled?

Remember how we'd milk the donkeys, those sad, bellowing donkeys, feeding the farm's production of ass-milk cheese, which none of the children wanted, though we ate it night and day, day and night, with snake eggs and donkey milk biscuits?

One thing I can't remember is how we ended up part of such a donkey-breeding, snake-handling hippie cult in the first place, or who we were before we arrived. Brother and sister? Cousins? Did we know each other at all before we were abducted and fell in love? Did we even exist? We must have, but I can't remember a time before you.

Remember the guard donkeys along the compound's periphery, protecting the sheep and ducks from the wolves and wild men roaming the countryside? Butch and his lover Priscilla were our favorites, because they would not stop braying and bellowing, would not guard anything, if separated. Remember the thrashings we'd endure at the hands of the humans, how I'd whisper to you from Edward Field's donkey poem late at night when we were finally alone: "They are not silent like work-horses / who are happy or indifferent about the plow and wagon / Donkeys don't submit like that. . . ."

And you'd whisper, "Laugh if you will when they hee-haw / But know that they are crying."

"Donkeys know what life should be," I'd say, still quoting Field, "But alas, they do not own their bodies."

We'd lay hands on each other then, kissing and braying like Butch and Priscilla, who did own their bodies at night. As did we. At night. No one can say we didn't own our bodies at night.

Remember the mud harvests? The bile mines?

Remember the potluck dinners, everyone wrapped in donkey hair blankets? All that fellowship and suffering. Everything we had to join and reject.

It's hard for me to remember anymore exactly what's true. I can't tell my memories from dreams now, my dreams from desires.

I do remember this, though. The smell of your skin and the lies we told to find each other. The necklace the river witch gave Mother Melanie to cure you of your forked tongue, a shimmering necklace that hung between your baby gazelle breasts, one bead of which would disappear for every lie you told. There must've been a thousand beads on that necklace, a wealth of lies we could not imagine spending.

This much is true, right? That there were guard donkeys out back, Butch and Priscilla, donkey lovers, because a lone donkey is a lonely donkey. That we fell in love on a cult compound where we served as bonded labor, beasts of burden. That there was a necklace around your neck, a collar waiting to choke you on our lies, and when the necklace grew tight, one disappearing bead away from asphyxiating you, you ran from the ass farm without telling me, knowing I would have run with you. I was young then. It never occurred to me that if you didn't leave, that if we were allowed to see each other from then on out forever, the lie that would one day kill you would be telling me we were still in love.

Remember the snakes in the spring house, testing the air with their tongues? Remember Priscilla kicking that dog to death, an old golden who wandered too close to the lamb pens? Remember kissing and shaking in the spring night, how we never got snake bit or donkey kicked? When they brought your blue body home, they left me alone for two days to roll in the mud and wail. But they didn't shoot me in the head, like they shot Butch when Priscilla had her stroke. He honked and hee-hawed for two days straight, never once leaving her dead donkey body, until Lance dropped him with a shot from his Browning T-Bolt. The silence that followed!

I like to think the lie that killed you was one you told yourself—that you'd be just fine without me. That's how small my love's become. I like to think we would have been as good and true as those donkeys had we stayed together. Remember how they honked and moaned the one time they were forced apart? They stomped and kicked and wheezed and wailed and would not do any work for those awful humans. Do you remember? How we handled snakes? How we'd drink whiskey and quote scripture and lay hands on each other? I need you to remember something, here. Anything. I can't tell what's true. All I remember is waiting for you and the sound of those donkeys howling.

DRUNK YOGA

Do you know what's better than hot yoga and power yoga and Bikram yoga and donkey yoga and that's guaranteed to become a major spiritual healing practice in about five seconds? Drunk yoga, that's what, also known as whiskey yoga or mindlessness yoga or you-still-seem-to-be-gaining-weight-but-who-cares yoga.

Imagine a class—let's call it Spirit Matters—offered through your local distillery/yoga studio with hundreds of 53-gallon charred oak barrels on racks in the back room. This place smells like a forest, but with trees full of booze, all kinds of whiskey here, Irish and single malt, bourbon and rye, our yoga mats scattered amongst the barrels and bottles just like when we were in kindergarten, and nap time was upon us. Booths line the periphery of our sacred space, selling jewelry and shoes and mala beads, nothing we need particularly, just stuff we want, nothing that will fill our bellies (aside from the small-plate offerings and salads and large-plate offerings and desserts) but food for the soul. Nobody needs a $278 free-trade natural poly blend yoga jacket, but we'd all be better off if we had one!

In Spirit Matters, the teachings of the great yogis—with modifications suiting our purposes—will illuminate our path to enlightenment. We'll study Rodney Yee's wisdom that "the most important pieces of equipment you need for doing yoga are your body and your mind." And maybe an Old Fashioned or two.

We'll embrace T. Guillemets' aphorism that "A photographer gets people to pose for him. A yoga instructor gets people to pose for themselves." But either way, you always seem to be posing. What's wrong with you?

We'll consider Sharon Gannon's observation that "You cannot do yoga. Yoga is your natural state. What you can do are yoga exercises." Or maybe you'd prefer a shot with a beer back, and some of these delicious hot wings—mild, spicy, or inferno!!!!

During class, we'll be mindful and drink cocktails. We'll discuss religion and politics, the idiot at the office, the idiot down the street, that fantastic new album by what's her name. We'll bond. We'll cleave apart. We'll argue. We'll heal! And then we'll put on our yoga pants and start posing—using modified standard positions. In drunk yoga, Downward Facing Dog becomes Downward Drunken Dog. Extended Hand to Big Toe becomes I Can't Do That at the Moment—I'm Mixing an Old Pal. Sun Salutation becomes You Guys Are So Awesome! Who's Got a

Cigarette? And One Legged King Pigeon becomes When You Really Get Down to it, When You Really Consider Why We're Here—Wait. What's Your Name Again? What Were You Just Saying?

Corpse pose will remain Corpse pose, but we're never going to do Corpse pose, even though some masters insist that it's the spiritual taproot, the mother of beauty. We've got other thoughts on that matter. Other taproots. We're not going to be quite that mindful. Ever. We're going to practice drunk yoga and we're going to be seen in Prohibition-nostalgic bars. We're going to sooth ourselves with spending and televised sports and drunk yoga. And when we tire of drunk yoga, we're going to invent other yogas, better yogas, Twitter yoga and tattoo yoga, save the children yoga and yoga for the criminally insane, fat yoga and skinny yoga, born-again yoga and barely born the first time yoga, a tired consumer's yoga, yoga for the shopped-out, sold-out, burned-out, blissed-out, all of us doing yoga all the time, grunting and sweating and breathing our way to the wholly whole.

Want to know if you're athletic enough, spiritual enough, flexible enough for drunk yoga? Try this at home: Have a drink and lie on the floor. Talk. Breathe. Silence yourself. Take a sip of your drink. Don't forget to breathe. If that proves too difficult, have a beer on the couch. Remember. Forget. Watch this channel, then that channel. Keep breathing. Sip your beer. Try another channel. Breathe.

We killed Kitty's husband with a harpoon her grandfather had given her, but it could have been a skillet or the steel ashtray from her kitchen table. The band would sit around that table at night, smoking and drinking and filling the house with music, and as it got late, Billy Wayne would make Kitty feel bad about who she was and what was best in her, calling her ignorant hillbilly trash and blaming her for everything that was small in him. He married her when she was fifteen, two months after he discovered her in Spokane, though everybody knew she didn't need to be discovered. She only needed to sing the sweet, sad songs we wrote, and America's heart would melt.

Our first single, "A Stone of Ice," told the story of Billy Wayne trampling Kitty's love with whiskey and womanizing, leaching all the goodness from her once pure soul. Every song we sang was about him. We wrote "This Bed You've Made" a month before he died, with the chorus that would make Kitty famous:

This bed you've made of cheating nights
This bed you've made of sin
This bed you've made of drunken lies
Is the bed I'm in with him

It broke our hearts to sing such mournful words, tears staining our cheeks as we wove our haunting hillbilly harmonies. We'd never even kissed, and here we were crying and singing and spitting in each other's faces, as close as we could get to kissing, since Billy Wayne's office was right beside the kitchen.

We sang it again. We sang it till Billy Wayne came out and stood before us with his arms across his chest. "Don't think I don't know what y'all are doing here," he said.

"We ain't doing nothing here," I said, and it was true, sort of.

"This song's gonna be a monster hit," I said.

"Don't tell me what's gonna be a monster hit," Billy Wayne said.

"Start it again, Blaze," Kitty said, and Billy Wayne stormed out the back door.

We sang it again, spitting all over each other, the air between us heavy and thick, our shiny faces inches apart, our voices ringing in the humid air. "I'm a married woman," Kitty said as I leaned in to kiss her. "A married woman," she said as we drove out the

70

Washburne road, sharing pulls from a bottle. "A woman on the edge," she said at the Wagon Wheel, where I hid my truck out back. "Oh, Blaze," she said as we rolled into bed, onto the floor, up against walls, all over that room.

Most folks don't realize how close a man and woman can get once they wake up to the fact of their own rotting. Kitty and I came alive through our wickedness for weeks, meeting at the Wagon Wheel and whispering beautiful, filthy things to each other.

"I'm a fallen woman," she said one afternoon, "no good to anyone."

"You're good to me," I said.

"Good as dead," she said. "He'll be coming for us."

And he did come, weeks later, slurring and wobbling into the kitchen where Kitty and I sat writing a song.

"You're drunk," Kitty said, and Billy Wayne said, "You're a harlot," and I said, "You can't call her that," and Billy Wayne said, "I can and I will."

I stood from the table, trying to loom.

He snarled, stumbling back to his office.

It felt good running him off like that, but he returned with Kitty's harpoon, charging her like a bull elephant.

I jumped from my chair and took him to the floor.

"This love's killing me!" he cried.

I put my knee to his back. "It's not love's gonna kill you!"

"My heart's a leaking sieve," he blubbered.

"A black and shriveled thing," I said.

"Please," he finally whimpered. "I just want my lonesome bed."

"Let him go," Kitty said, and we watched him crawl out of the kitchen.

"Awful," she said, "what love can do."

"That ain't love," I said, and Kitty said, "Don't tell me what love is, Blaze," and Billy Wayne burst into the kitchen with his Navy Colt revolver.

I grabbed the harpoon from the floor. Billy Wayne fired and I harpooned him through the side, then twisted into his heart and lungs, killing him deader than hell. The righteousness I felt as he dropped to the floor, burbling and bleeding, Kitty beside him crying tears of joy and love and hatred! I picked her up so she wouldn't be stained by his leakage. "Oh, baby," she said, as I kissed her and petted her. "Oh, darling," she said, as she ran her hands over me. There was no doubt that she was mine and I was hers, that no one in the world would tear us asunder. You can't get closer than killing for love. In fact, you'll never get that close again, though you'll think it's all just beginning.

At the Wagon Wheel, we wrapped ourselves around each other for days, free and gorging, until Kitty started making herself famous, returning phone calls to the newspapers and record labels. You probably know that room as 319, from our monster hit, "That's Not Love Leaking From the Harpoon Hole in Your Heart," but there was no Room 319. The Wagon Wheel had just thirteen rooms, each a shrine to the love we shared when we were writing monster hits nobody knew—"This Bed You've Made," and "Whiskey Tears," and "(If You're) Here for Love (Come Back When You're Dead and Gone)." Those songs proved our love, were our love. Everything was our love. Even our hatred. Even our fear. Even the harpoon we killed Billy Wayne with. We'd be burning with it still, if only we had Billy Wayne to hate and hide from and murder forever. If only we'd been arrested and sentenced to death. But the police couldn't let us go fast enough. Everyone knew Billy Wayne deserved that harpoon. But nobody deserves love. Or everyone does. It comes and it goes of its own free will. Like fever. Like flood. Like the greatest thing you're ever gonna lose, whether you harpoon a man or not. Oh, Kitty, my baby darling! And once it's gone, it's gone for good.

The maid's nose was snipped off by a blackbird while she was hanging clothes in the garden. I didn't see it, having just walked away from the window upstairs, but there were plenty of witnesses, and while one claimed her nose was pecked off, and another claimed it was snapped off, and the maid herself, before bleeding to death, said it had definitely been snipped off, the essence of the thing remained the same. My beautiful Tammy was attacked by a blackbird while hanging laundry in the garden. This was after the pie was opened, after the king had turned to the bottle, and the queen to one of her young lovers. It was a pattern with them, part of the reason for all the laundry— the king soiling his robes and pantaloons, the queen binging and purging and fornicating all over the castle. They were horrible people, the king and queen. What do you expect? Treat people like gods and they'll behave like swine. But I'm talking about Tammy here, my one true love, disfigured and wailing out in the garden.

Had the physician been able to stop her bleeding, I'd have gone on loving Tammy, with or without a nose. Without eyes, I'd have loved her. Without ears or a chin, ankles or elbows, propped on a straw bed for three and ninety years, I'd have worshipped Tammy. Had an eagle swooped down and pecked off her buttocks, severing her legs and causing them to fall from her body, I'd have braved fire, eaten rocks, tamed demons for the love of Tammy's torso. Had she but lived.

The king was in the counting house, counting out his money. Do you see what I'm saying about these people? The king had a separate building for his money, brick and stone, while the rest of us lived in mud-daubed hovels. He kept a flask in his robes filled with rye, and I'd hear him grunting and muttering drunkenly in the counting house as he slobbered over his gold.

The queen was in the parlor, eating bread and honey. She could never get enough, and after she ate, she purged, and after she purged, she'd slather one of her boys with lard or butter, or wrap him in a string of sausages for more binging. Sometimes she'd nip at a finger or toe, but she hadn't started eating her lovers yet. Not in earnest. The way she examined their haunches, though, poking and prodding, you knew it was only a matter of time. This is what I mean about these people, why somebody had to stop them.

It took two years to train the birds. Tammy thought we should use poison, but I wanted drama, the bold statement. "Jackdaws, then," she said. "Or ravens. The ghosts of the murdered dead to peck out their eyes." But it was blackbirds I wanted, the sweetness of their song. I did what I did for love, for Tammy. I did what I did for hatred, too. I did what I did as the one grand gesture of my life.

"Poetry must have something in it barbaric, vast, and wild," Tammy would say to me, quoting Diderot, as we lay in our bed of dung, happy in spite of our loathing for our lords and ladies. I'd quote Diderot right back to her: "Hang the last king by the guts of the last priest," and we'd make wild pagan love until morning. Say what you will about bile and simmering rage, but our hatred for our betters bound us as much as anything. I loved Tammy for the murder in her heart as much as for her club foot or cleft palate. We were the ones who should have been royal—or so much more than royal—not a baker and scullery maid, but gods, wrathful and glorious, emerging from the sun dripping fire.

When the pie was opened, the birds began to sing, one tentative whistle and then another and then a keening chorus as they came to life inside the vented crust. The flurry that followed was the most startling thing I've ever witnessed, all my dreams of murder come to life on explosive black wings. I thought of Diderot's words, "Only great passions can elevate the soul to great things." I thought of Tammy in the garden, waiting for night, our furious love and hatred, our plotting and scheming, training those birds, and now the magic of their rising on wafts of steam, a flurry of feather and birdsong and gasps from the royal fuck-faces as the birds prepared to peck through their eyes and into their worm-infested brains. The glory of it all!

But those fucking birds. Do you know what happened? They flew straight up and out the windows. That's what happened.

After all that shrieking and flapping, the air fairly crackled. How horribly wrong it had all gone. Instead of a new life for Tammy and me, I would be led to the block for beheading. Or more likely, I'd be disemboweled, then beheaded, and finally quartered, while Tammy would go on without me, quoting Diderot to somebody else.

The king hit his flask. "Nicely done," he said to me. "Jim, is it?

I looked up from the floor. "Bob," I said.

"Bravo, Bob," the king said, toasting me with his flask and taking another long pull.

"Wasn't that a dainty dish," the queen said, reaching for the pie pan and stuffing her gob with fistfuls of birdshit and crumbling crust.

"Come on, Elizabeth," the king said. "We're not supposed to eat that."

"Of course we're supposed to eat it," the queen said.

"I'm going to the counting house," the king said, but the queen ignored him. I walked to the window and saw my Tammy in the garden below. The queen filled her pie hole. Maybe we'd find another way to set ourselves free. Outside, the blackbirds wheeled against a perfect blue sky. One pulled away from the others and circled on extended wings, drifting slowly, silently, down, down, down.

ACKNOWLEDGMENTS

"A Prayer for My Neighbor's Quick, Painless Death" first appeared in *A Book of Uncommon Prayer*. San Francisco: Outpost 19, 2015.

"Down on the Ass Farm" first appeared in *The Normal School,* February 2016

"Drunk Yoga" first appeared as "Spirit Matters" in *The Inlander*, 11 March 2015.

"Exxon, My Love" first appeared in *Fugue 45,* Fall 2013.

"Glazed" first appeared in *The Flash: An Anthology of Short Fiction*. London: Social Disease, 2007.

"Paradise Lost" first appeared in *Hobart*, Spring 2015.

"Pie & Whiskey" first appeared in *Prairie Schooner* 89:1, Spring 2015.

"Professor Astor's Unsolicited Blurb" first appeared in *The Official Catalogue of the Library of Potential Literature*. New York: Cow Heavy Books, 2011.

"Sing a Song of Sixpence" first appeared in *Okey-Panky*, December 2015.

"The Little Goat" first appeared in *Lilac City Fairy Tales*, 2014 and *New World Writing,* February 2016.

"This Bed You've Made" first appeared in *New Ohio Review 18,* Fall 2015.

"Wonderland" first appeared in *The Spokesman-Review,* 10 August 2014.

SAMUEL LIGON is the author of two novels, *Among the Dead and Dreaming* and *Safe in Heaven Dead,* and a collection of stories, *Drift and Swerve.* His short fiction has appeared in *Prairie Schooner, New England Review, New Ohio Review, Gulf Coast,* and elsewhere. Ligon edits the journal *Willow Springs,* teaches at Eastern Washington University in Spokane, and is the artistic director of the Port Townsend Writers' Conference.

STEPHEN KNEZOVICH is a writer, editor, and artist living in Philadelphia, Pennsylvania. He is the director of marketing and publicity for *Creative Nonfiction* magazine, In Fact Books, and the Creative Nonfiction Foundation's educational programs. He earned an MFA in Creative Writing from Eastern Washington University.